Published Author

INKLET #66

LIANA BROOKS

Inkprint PRESS
www.inkprintpress.com

Print ISBN: 978-1-925825-68-8
eBook ISBN: 9798201573263

www.inkprintpress.com

National Library of Australia Cataloguing-in-Publication Data
Brooks, Liana 1983 –
Published Author
40 p.
ISBN: 978-1-925825-68-8
Inkprint Press, Canberra, Australia
1. Fiction—Fantasy—Contemporary 2. Fiction—Short Stories

First Print Edition: September 2021
Cover photo © Conger Design via Pixabay
Cover design © Inkprint Press
Interior art © Amy Laurens

Published Author

LIANA BROOKS

OTHER WORKS

ALL I WANT FOR CHRISTMAS

All I Want For Christmas Is A Reaper
All I Want For Christmas Is A Werewolf

FLEET OF MALIK

Bodies In Motion
Change of Momentum

HEROES AND VILLAINS

Even Villains Fall In Love
Even Villains Go To The Movies
Even Villains Have Interns
Even Villains Play The Hero (books 1 – 3 omnibus)
The Polar Terror

TIME AND SHADOWS

The Day Before
Convergence Point
Decoherence

SHORTER WORKS

Fey Lights
Prime Sensations
Darkness and Good

Find other works by the author at
www.lianabrooks.com

PUBLISHED AUTHOR

Horace Jones chewed his lip as he rode the elevator up seven floors to his Manhattan apartment. At the door, he hesitated. Was it really over? He eased the door open and peered into the dark. "Hello? Domino?"

His black-and-white terrier-something ran toward him, ears perked.

"Is it safe?" Horace asked as he flipped on the light.

Domino thumped his stubby tail on the wood floor.

"All right then."

Slamming the door, Horace secured the lock and scanned the near-empty living room: one couch, one table, one chair, one empty bookshelf.

The dog ran to the couch, barking. His tail knocked the table. A piece of paper fluttered gently to the ground.

"No!" Horace threw himself down, sobbing. His fists beat the hardwood floor and hot tears streaked down his face. "No! Not again!"

Domino whined in confusion.

Defeated, Horace crawled forward. With trembling hands he lifted up the paper, dreading what he would see...

"A bill! Oh, thank all my lucky stars, a bill! Look!" He shoved the bill from the dog-walker in Domino's face, laughing giddily. "A bill!" He rushed to the bookshelf to check the layer of dust. "Empty!"

Horace collapsed on his plush red couch, smiling at the empty shelves. "No one understands, Domino. They don't know the burden I live with." But the bookshelf remained empty. For the first time in weeks he felt safe, completely at peace with himself.

Domino put his nose on the couch, brown eyes gazing up with total adoration.

"Right, food. Let's see what we'll have for dinner, shall we?" Horace hit his legs with forced enthusiasm and stood up, rubbing his face. "The gala today was awful. All those flashes, five microphones shoved right up my nose. My mouth positively aches from smiling. I mean really," he addressed the dog, "how many questions can you have about a book? I'm a private person! I want a private life! Is that too much to ask?"

Tail thumping expectantly, Domino sat at his food dish.

Horace opened the fridge. Leftovers from the week were piled in front, while older dinners lurked in the back, enjoying complicated lives of their own. "I have steak tartar left from the dinner with Jay Leno yesterday. Cake left over from the buffet with Ellen the day before. And something pasta left from the lunch with Oprah that I went to on Monday. What would you like?"

A bark and a growl.

"Steak it is." Horace emptied the Styrofoam box into the dog's dish. "Eat up." He pulled a leftover sandwich from the back of the fridge and read the scribbled handwriting. "Writer's conference? When did we last go to a writer's conference?"

With a steak in front of him, Domino was too distracted to comment.

"Probably not good for me then." Horace tossed it in the trash. He looked back in the fridge and, with a shrug, tossed the rest of the leftover food as well.

Domino whimpered, covering his eyes with his paw.

"We'll go shopping tomorrow," Horace promised.

He pulled a candy bar out of the vegetable drawer. "Cold, but tasty!"

The dog growled at him.

"It's healthy!" Horace protested. "It has peanuts."

He sat down beside Domino on the floor and watched the mutt enjoy his steak. Being a dog certainly looked nice. Easier than being a best-selling author at least.

While his sixth book in three years was breaking earning records, Horace worried.

The New York Times couldn't get enough of him. His agent, who had started three years ago with a client list of one, was now the most sought after agent in New York. She still kept a client list of one.

And the Most Successful Agent expected her one client to keep her wealthy. When Evil Editor Madeline called Most Successful Agent demanding to know when the next bestseller was going to be on her desk, Most Successful Agent would turn to him.

Horace covered his face with his hands.

If he were lucky, very lucky, that sixth book would be his last. Maybe then all this would go away and he could fade into obscurity. He hadn't *meant* for things to get out of control like this. It had been a joke, a way to needle his friends at the coffee shop by showing them his finished manuscript while they slaved away at their own editing.

Querying had been a fun game... Until the agents started calling. Then everything had snowballed and there hadn't been a chance to explain the joke to anyone but Domino.

He peeked through the kitchen doorway at the bookshelf.

It remained empty.

Maybe the nightmare was ending.

"Come on," he said, patting the dog. "Let's go take our showers and get some sleep. Our devoted agent will be calling in the morning, bright and early, to drag me off to another interview. Wouldn't want to look tired."

He stumbled off to shower, avoiding the mirror. He was over fifty and he hadn't aged well. His PR people didn't care; they told him he looked affable and jovial. Horace considered that over-kind. He was middle-aged, over-weight, balding, and had bad teeth. But he never posed for the cover of the books, so it didn't matter.

He shaved, letting Domino play in the shower water while it warmed. He shooed the dog out, washed, and groped around for his towel. And groped some more, dripping water on the floor. "Blast!" He scurried into the air-conditioned hall, shivering; ran to the linen closet to grope there for a towel… He pulled out a manuscript.

"Domino!!" His shriek brought the dog running. "Domino, we've been attacked!"

The dog skidded to a halt on the wet floor and looked up at his dripping master.

Horace shook the manuscript.

Domino's ears flattened and his tail tucked under.

Horace held out the book. "Try chewing it a bit?"

Domino yelped and ran.

"Coward!" Horace threw the infernal manuscript into the puddle of water and left it there while he dried.

Determined not to endure a seventh run as the New York Times' best-selling author, he paraded past the manuscript to his room. He pulled on flannel pajamas, hands shaking as he did up the buttons.

A quick peek around corner confirmed that the manuscript hadn't vanished.

He cleaned the bathroom, then scrubbed the toilet, disinfected the dog's dish, and finally hung a dry towel by the shower.

The manuscript hadn't moved.

Fear growing by the moment, he tided the house, dusting, mopping, straightening... Realizing he'd run out of all possible chores except mopping up the puddle with the manuscript, he picked up the unwanted pages.

Times New Roman, twelve-point font, double-spaced. Just the way his agent liked it.

The water hadn't even ruined the edges.

"Blast!"

Shuddering, he slumped back to the bedroom, turned on the bedside light, and sat down to read the book.

Domino hopped up beside him for moral support.

"Look at this first page!" Horace wailed. "It's perfect!"

Gripping, intense, passionate...

"The New York Times are going to rave about this, I know it." Tears blurred his vision.

He tried page two. Perfect.

Page three was even better.

"I know what the New York Times will say," he said with a sniffle. "'A brilliant masterpiece of cunning wit, enduring love, and a timeless metaphor for the human condition.' They have done that to me before."

Horace sobbed.

Domino played dead.

"We have to get rid of this. I can't face another book signing. I can't go on Oprah again! No more parties! No more reviews! I can't stand the pressure!"

He looked down at the dog.

"We burn it. No one will ever know. I'll fade into comfortable obscurity. I won't go insane and you won't have to live in the pound with cats. No one will ever know that I can't write to save my life. We end it. Tonight."

Domino followed him to the living room and watched him start the fire.

"It's for the best," Horace promised.

He tossed the manuscript in and watched. The fire merrily burned away around the book. Flames kissed the manuscript. Hot breezes rifled the pages. Burning logs popped in accolade. But the pages didn't singe.

"This is a nightmare!" Horace threw another log on the fire and ran to hide under his blankets, praying the manuscript would turn to ash in the morning sunlight like the life-sucking vampire it was.

All through the night he tossed and turned. Awards shows haunted his dreams. Hollywood directors calling for movie rights turned angry when he couldn't remember the characters' names…

The next morning his sheets were drenched in sweat. The smell of animal fear permeated the room.

A key clicked in the lock of the apartment. His agent! He had to hide the manuscript before she found it!

Horace stumbled into the living room, bleary eyed and nauseous with worry.

His perfectly groomed agent perched on the couch devouring the latest—unsinged—manuscript.

"Horace! This is brilliant!" She gave him a very stern look. "Why was it in the fireplace?"

"Oh, uh, well, you know how I feel about first drafts." He gave her a weak smile. The future loomed dark with the promise of lies and television appearances. He would tell her. Right now, he'd confess that he hadn't written the book. She could make everything go away.

But she laughed, smiling up at him as if he could do no wrong. "I don't know how you do it."

Resolve crumpled. Horace echoed her with a nervous laugh of his own. "The books just... come to me. Isn't that how it works for everyone?"

THE MAKING OF
PUBLISHED AUTHOR

Once upon a time a very frustrated young author daydreamed about how Bestsellers came to be.

They seemed to appear out of the ether. Magically and spontaneously erupting out of aged writing desks, like the kind of fungus that a 15th-century scholar would use as definitive proof of spontaneous generation.

I thought that if such a thing happened to me, I would be very tempted to take the credit. Most authors would be—at least a little.

But what would happen after that?

What would happen if you built your career not on your own skill, but on the whim of miraculously appearing novels?

It seemed to me that perhaps that wouldn't be such a good thing after all.

Read more by Liana Brooks!

EVEN VILLAINS
FALL IN LOVE

CHAPTER ONE

I knew from the first time I saw my wife that I wanted her naked. Of course, seven minutes later I wanted revenge. It wasn't that she had handed me my first defeat or ruined my chances for world domination that year, it was the way she kissed me good-bye. She sent my head spinning, then walked away as if I were the least important person in the world.

Once my arm healed, I stole some new equipment, cloned some new minions, and I felt a little different.

I wanted revenge, with a side order of naked.

ACROSS THE DINNER table, Tabitha devoured him with dark, ocean-blue eyes. She put a bite of lettuce in her mouth, full lips pursing around it. Eating salad never looked so good. Her tongue darted out to lick away a stray drop of dressing. She winked at him, promising with every move to do the same to him. "It's almost bedtime," she said, her voice husky and luscious.

"I don't wanna go to bed!" one of the quads screamed.

"What about cake? Don't we get birthday cake?" another asked.

Evan winked back at his wife from the far side of the table, separated by a few feet and four precocious just-turned-five-year olds, all as stunning as their mother with big, round eyes and hair that fell in loose curls meant to trap hairbrushes and sticky substances.

He had to peek at the eyes to see who was talking. Maria had green eyes, Angela's eyes were blue like Tabitha's, Delilah's eyes were brown like his, and Blessing—their stillborn who miraculously survived—had purple eyes. The waif in question had blue eyes.

"Angela," Evan said, "after dinner it's pajama time, and then story time."

"Mommy doesn't have a bedtime!" Angela wailed.

Tabitha winked at him again. "Tell you what, tonight Mommy will go to bed the same time you do. Right after we eat cake." She leaned over to give Angela a hug.

All Evan could see was the deep V plunge of her tight blue shirt. Oh, yeah. Crime didn't always pay, but altering someone's moral compass sure put the O's back in the bedroom.

The cake was split into fourths, equal parts purple, white, green, and blue so each girl could have her favorite color in the cake.

Baking four cakes was unreasonable; there weren't any grandparents left to celebrate with, and neighbors had an annoying habit of asking uncomfortable questions. Saying little things like, "You look just like Doctor Charm! Do you remember him? Whatever happened to that guy? Do you know how hard it is to put together a good Villains vs. Heroes fantasy league without him?" made for awkward evenings.

So they had a quiet family party. Cake, then presents, after which he hurried the girls off to bed so he could read Dilly Duck's ABCs in record time before rushing to the bedroom, hoping to catch Tabitha still in the shower.

She was already out and wearing a blue satin robe that caressed her skin in exactly the way he wanted to. Rose-scented candles cast sensuous shadows on the walls.

Tabitha turned, lips curved in an inviting smile. Long fingers twined with the sash of her robe. She tossed her honey-blonde hair in the way she always did when she was about to argue, posing with feet apart and one hand casually resting on her waist. "Sweetie, we need to talk."

Evan wiped grease-stained hands on his jeans as he forced a smile. "Sure, babes, anything you want."

"Really?" She slunk forward, all sinewy limbs and doe eyes. "Promise?" Tabitha nuzzled his nose. One hand flirted up the back of his neck to play with his hair. The other traveled downward, right to his zipper.

Oh, yes, the little Morality Machine in the basement was working just fine. Another thirty, maybe forty years of this and he'd consider retiring.

Or turning the machine down so his wife wasn't quite a sex kitten every day of the week.

Maybe only days with Y in them.

"Sweetie?" She nibbled his ear. "I want to go back to work."

"What?" Evan actually pushed himself away from her, something he wasn't sure was possible in any other circumstance.

Tabitha tucked her chin and pouted.

"Tabby-cat, I love you, but work? I've got my... stuff... in the lab. I'm busy. And we can't afford daycare for the girls. We're barely making ends meet as it is. Do you really want to go back to being Zephyr Girl? Crime fighting is a game for the young, baby. You're not nineteen anymore."

"I'm twenty-nine. A very"—her hips pressed against his tight jeans just so—"very healthy twenty-nine."

He shivered at her touch. "You're cheating."

"I want to do this, Evan." She ground against the thick denim.

"You can do me all you want, baby."

She stepped back, frowning. "I'm serious."

"So am I." Evan sighed, reaching for his wife. "Sweetie, I love you, but what's the point in being a superhero?

The government stipend barely covers the dry-cleaning bill. If it's money you want, write another tell-all superhero book. The Spanish Mask sold his third last month."

Tabitha crossed her arms. "I don't want to write another book just for royalties while you're between jobs."

He waved a finger at her. "I'm not between jobs. I work freelance in the computer business. I'm self-employed. That's not the same as being between jobs."

"Between paychecks then."

"We will have a solid income. This project I'm working on, Tabby-cat, it's going to set us up for life. We're never going to worry about money again. I promise. Give me a couple of weeks and everything is going to be perfect." He caught her hand and pulled her into his arms. The faint scent of her spicy perfume left him dizzy with need.

She rested her head on his chest. "I

want to save the world. Have you seen the news, Evan? An entire town in Kansas held hostage for a week by a bomb scare before a superhero was able to get in to defuse the situation. A week! I could have that done between grocery shopping and paying the bills. Ten minutes, no pulling punches."

"I know, baby. No one is better at this stuff than you. But I need you at home, Tabby. Having you out there scares me. I'm terrified I'd lose you. Why don't you wait until I finish this project? I'll be done by the time the election rolls around. Two more weeks. Once I get paid we'll look at this again. I have that armor design for you, I just need some time to put it together."

Tabitha sighed. "You've been saying that since we got married."

"Well, my nights are busy." He nibbled her ear as he tugged her sash loose. "Are you complaining?"

Tabitha stretched against him, sending a delightful frisson of lust up his spine. "I thought you gave up the super villain schemes."

He twitched. "I did, baby. Of course I did."

"But you're keeping me here. Isn't that a little selfish? Just a teeny-tiny bit super villain-ish?" She slipped her hand between his pants and his skin.

"Ah!" He caught her hand so he could think clearly. "Not selfish. Necessary. Like oxygen or sex."

"Don't you mean water?"

"No, definitely sex." Evan slid her robe off and tossed it into a corner. "Come here, Tabby-cat, I'll make you purr."

She tugged at his shirt, pulling it up. The shirt joined the robe on the other side of the room. "What are you doing down in that lab?" she asked as her hands drew lazy circles on his back.

Ten seconds, that's all he'd need to

get her panties off. Three more to drop his pants. "What was the question?"

"What are you doing in the lab? What's this project?"

"Oh, computer stuff. I told you. To help tally everything on election night. I'm trying to make the process run smoother so we don't have to worry about recounts."

"Hmmm." She gave him a dubious frown.

Tabitha was built like a supermodel and had a superhero name straight from Campy Comics, but her brain was Mensa all the way. "And this computer program has nothing to do with world domination, or get-rich-quick schemes?"

Evan contrived to look wounded. "Tabby-cat, how can you ask that?"

"Because you spent ten years as a villainous criminal mastermind?"

"I wasn't a mastermind, I was a super villain, there's a difference. Masterminds are just thugs with money. My crimes had artistic flare. I was practically Robin Hood! Robbing from the rich and scandalous, and giving to me."

"Robin Hood gave to the poor," Tabitha said with a laugh. "You were never poor."

He caught her hand, pulling her close. "Poor is relative. Besides, I'm reformed now. You showed me the error of my wicked ways. Although"— he leaned in for a kiss—"if you'd like to remind me why I gave up a lucrative life of crime, I have the evening free."

Keep reading! Head to
www.inkprintpress.com/
lianabrooks/heroesandvillains
/love/
to buy your copy now!

ABOUT THE AUTHOR

LIANA BROOKS has often tried leaving books to write themselves. She hasn't had much luck so far, so she's been forced to do some typing. This has resulted in a wide range of stories, from sprawling space operas (*Fleet of Malik*) to the antics of a superhero family (*Heroes and Villains*). Liana also writes the *All I Want For Christmas* novellas.

You can learn more about her and her books at www.LianaBrooks.com.

INKLETS

Collect them all! Released on the
1st and 15th of each month.

INKLET #055
Allure
AMY LAURENS

INKLET #056
The LIES We KNOW
LIANA BROOKS

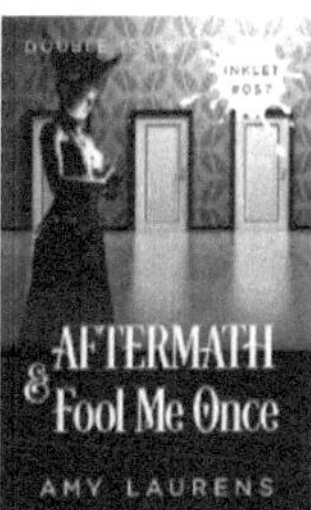

INKLET #057
AFTERMATH & Fool Me Once
AMY LAURENS

INKLET #058
Purity
An Age Of Unicorns Story
AMY LAURENS

INKLET #059
Saved
AMY LAURENS

INKLET #060
A Kiss is the Secret
AMY LAURENS

INKLET #061
A Changing Tides Story
Fire Bright
AMY LAURENS

INKLET #062
Hades AND Persephone
LIANA BROOKS

INKLET #063
Just So Long As You're Happy
AMY LAURENS

INKLET #064
Theft Of A Lifetime
LIANA BROOKS

INKLET #065
Shoe
AMY LAURENS

INKLET #066
Published AUTHOR
LIANA BROOKS

DOUBLE ISSUE
INKLET #067
THE REMARKABLE INSIGHT OF JELLYBEANS & Understanding
AMY LAURENS

INKLET #068
Desperate Measures
AMY LAURENS

INKLET #069
Rock-a-bye
LIANA BROOKS

INKLET #070
the Other Carly
AMY LAURENS

INKLET #071
Bs By Bioluminescent light
AMY LAURENS

INKLET #072
Even Villains Grant Wishes
A Heroes & Villains Story
LIANA BROOKS

www.ingramcontent.com/pod-product-compliance
Lightning Source LLC
Chambersburg PA
CBHW030813190726
48285CB00003B/1157